Who is following Cam and Eric?

As Cam and Eric walked past a large wooded area, Cam heard the sounds of twigs breaking.

"Did you hear anything?" Cam asked Eric.

"No."

Cam heard the sounds of twigs breaking again.

"Did you hear that?" Cam whispered.

"Yes. It sounds like something moving in the woods. Maybe it's an animal."

"It's not an animal," Cam whispered. "An animal wouldn't stop whenever we do. Someone is following us."

THE CAM JANSEN ADVENTURE SERIES
David A. Adler/Susanna Natti

Cam Jansen and the Mystery of the Stolen Diamonds
Cam Jansen and the Mystery of the U.F.O.
Cam Jansen and the Mystery of the Dinosaur Bones
Cam Jansen and the Mystery of the Television Dog
Cam Jansen and the Mystery of the Gold Coins
Cam Jansen and the Mystery of the Babe Ruth Baseball
Cam Jansen and the Mystery of the Circus Clown
Cam Jansen and the Mystery of the Monster Movie
Cam Jansen and the Mystery of the Carnival Prize
Cam Jansen and the Mystery at the Monkey House
Cam Jansen and the Mystery of the Stolen Corn Popper
Cam Jansen and the Mystery of Flight 54
Cam Jansen and the Mystery at the Haunted House
Cam Jansen and the Chocolate Fudge Mystery
Cam Jansen and the Triceratops Pops Mystery
Cam Jansen and the Ghostly Mystery
Cam Jansen and the Scary Snake Mystery

CAM JANSEN

and the
Mystery of the
Gold Coins

CAM JANSEN

and the
Mystery of the
Gold Coins

★ ★

DAVID A. ADLER
Illustrated by Susanna Natti

★ ★

PUFFIN BOOKS

PUFFIN BOOKS

Published by the Penguin Group

Penguin Putnam Inc., 375 Hudson Street, New York, New York 10014, U.S.A.

Penguin Books Ltd, 27 Wrights Lane, London W8 5TZ, England

Penguin Books Australia Ltd, Ringwood, Victoria, Australia

Penguin Books Canada Ltd, 10 Alcorn Avenue, Toronto, Ontario, Canada M4V 3B2

Penguin Books (N.Z.) Ltd, 182-190 Wairau Road, Auckland 10, New Zealand

Penguin Books Ltd, Registered Offices: Harmondsworth, Middlesex, England

First published in the United States of America by Viking Penguin Inc., 1982
Published in Puffin Books, 1991
Reissued 1998

5 7 9 10 8 6

THE LIBRARY OF CONGRESS HAS CATALOGED THE PREVIOUS PUFFIN BOOKS EDITION
UNDER CATALOG CARD NUMBER: 91-53036

This edition ISBN 0-14-038954-7

Printed in the United States of America

RL: 2.2

To My Niece, Shira,
And To Her Parents,
Felice and Mark

Chapter One

Cam Jansen and her friend Eric Shelton were carrying their science fair projects to school. Cam had made a box camera. Eric's project was a big, heavy wooden sundial.

Cam looked at Eric. His face was turning red.

"I think we should stop here and rest," Cam said.

"No. I can go a little farther."

Eric took a few more steps. Then the sundial started to slip from his hands.

"O.K.," Eric said. "We can rest now if you want to."

They were standing close to a bus stop. Eric put the sundial down quickly, before it could fall. Then he sat on the bus stop bench. Cam sat next to him. She put the black cloth bag she was holding on her lap. The camera was inside the bag.

"You didn't have to make your sundial so big," Cam said.

"I made it big so we could put it in the garden after the science fair. My mother said she'll plant ivy around it."

Eric looked at the cloth bag Cam was holding and asked, "What are you going to do with your camera?"

"I'll keep it, of course."

"Why? Your mental camera takes better pictures than any real camera. And your mental camera never needs film."

Cam's mental camera is her memory. She can look at a scene and remember every detail. It's as if she had a photograph of the scene stored in her mind.

Whenever Cam wants to remember something, she looks at it carefully and says, *"Click."* Cam says *"Click"* is the sound her mental camera makes when it takes a picture.

When Cam was younger, people called her Jennifer—that's her real name—and "Red," because she has red hair. But when they found out about her photographic memory and heard her say, *"Click,"* they started calling her "The Camera." Soon "The Camera" was shortened to "Cam."

"I know that my mental camera doesn't need film," Cam told Eric, "but I can't show people the photographs stored in my brain. And I can't put my mental photographs in an album. So I need a real camera, too."

Just then a bus stopped. A young couple got off. They looked at Eric's project.

"What's that?" the man asked.

"It's a sundial."

"Can it really tell time?" the woman asked.

"Sure. If the arrow is pointed north and the sun is shining."

"And you carry that around all the time," the man said. He laughed. "It must be heavy. Wouldn't it be easier to wear a wristwatch?"

Eric started to explain that the sundial

was for the fifth grade science fair. But the man wasn't listening.

"I should have asked him how he winds it, or if it tells time underwater," the man said to the woman as they walked away, laughing.

"Let's go," Cam said to Eric, "before someone asks you what time it is."

Eric stood behind his sundial. He straightened his collar and smiled.

"First take my picture."

Cam stepped back a few feet. She looked straight at Eric and said, *"Click."*

"No. Use your real camera."

It was a bright spring day. The sun was behind Cam. "With this camera, you have to stand perfectly still for five seconds," she told Eric. "If you move, the picture will be a blur."

Cam took the camera from the bag. She held it with both hands. She pulled a string that lifted a cardboard flap. Then she counted, "One Mississippi, two Mississippi, three Mississippi, four Mississippi, five Mississippi." She let the string go and the flap fell down again.

"Do you think it will come out?" Eric asked.

"If I aimed the camera right, you'll come out. You stood still. But behind you will be a blur. A car drove past. A man came out of one of the stores, and someone walked by with a dog."

9

As Cam put the camera in its bag, a young man in a red plaid jacket ran past. He knocked into Cam. Her camera fell, and the man bent down to pick it up. But Eric had it.

"It's lucky I caught this before it hit the ground," Eric said. "It might have broken."

Cam wasn't listening. She was watching the man run off. "He must be in some rush," she said. "He didn't even say he was sorry."

Chapter Two

Cam put her camera back in the bag. Eric picked up his sundial, and they walked together toward school.

As they walked past a large wooded area, Cam heard the sounds of twigs breaking. Eric stopped walking so he could rest. Cam stopped, too. So did the sounds. Cam turned around, but no one was there.

"Did you hear anything?" Cam asked Eric.

"No."

Eric said he was ready. He picked up the

sundial, and he and Cam began to walk. Cam heard the sounds of twigs breaking again.

"Did you hear that?" Cam whispered.

"Yes. It sounds like something moving in the woods. Maybe it's an animal."

"Stop for a minute."

Eric put down the sundial, and the sounds of footsteps stopped.

"It's not an animal," Cam whispered.

"An animal wouldn't stop whenever we do. Someone is following us."

"Why would anyone follow us?" Eric asked.

"I don't know. But let's not stay here and find out! Can you run with that thing?"

"I'll try."

Eric picked up the sundial. He tried to run, but his knees kept hitting the sundial. He and Cam stopped at the corner. Cam turned, but she didn't see anyone behind them. Then Cam and Eric crossed the street and ran the one block to school. They went in through the side entrance. When they got inside, Eric dropped the sundial and collapsed on the floor.

"Were we followed here?" he asked. He was out of breath.

"I don't know. I don't see anyone out there," Cam said.

Cam waited while Eric rested. Then they went together to the auditorium. Near the door a teacher was sitting behind a desk.

"I'm Jennifer Jansen and this is Eric Shelton. Where should we put our science projects?"

The teacher looked at Cam for a moment. Then she said, "Are you the girl Ms. Benson told me about, the one with the amazing memory?"

"Yes, she is," Eric said. "We call her Cam, and she remembers everything. Just watch."

Eric told Cam to look at the teacher and say, *"Click."*

Cam looked at the teacher. She said, *"Click,"* and closed her eyes.

"Now ask Cam anything," Eric said. "Ask her what color your hair is or what it says on that button you're wearing."

"All right. What does the button say?" the teacher asked.

Cam's eyes were still closed. She said, "You're wearing a lot of buttons. The cam-

paign button you have on your collar says,
'Vote Smart. Ed Smart for Senator.' The
buttons on your dress say GGC for Gully,
Gully Clothes. And the second button from
the top is chipped."

The teacher looked at her second button.
"It *is* chipped," she said. "Amazing. Well,
it's a real pleasure to meet you, Jennifer."

The teacher looked at a list she had on
her desk and said, "Jennifer, you can set

up your project on table 54. Eric, you can set your project up next to table 48."

Cam and Eric walked into the school auditorium.

"Look over there," Eric said. "Linda Baker is talking to Ms. Benson. I'll bet she's telling Ms. Benson how great her project is. She'd do anything to win."

Cam said, "Let's set up our projects. Then we can look at what Linda and everyone else made."

Cam went to table 54. She took her camera, two folders, and some tape from the bag she was holding. Cam opened the folders and taped them to the table. The first folder explained how Cam had made the camera. The second folder had some photographs Cam had taken with the camera. Cam put her camera between the two folders and went to find Eric.

Eric was looking at Linda Baker's project. It was called "Light Helps Plants

Grow." There were a few pots with different-size plants growing in them and with signs saying how many hours of light each plant got each day. One pot was empty. The sign in the empty pot said, "Zero."

"How do you like my project?" Linda asked. "Ms. Benson said it was very well done."

LIGHT ☼ HELPS PLANTS ✿ GROW

TABLE 33

"It's very nice," Cam said.

Linda smiled. "I think it's going to win. I'll get a science trophy just like my brother did."

As they walked away, Eric whispered to Cam, "I'll bet Linda never watered the plants that she didn't want to grow. She'd do anything to win."

Cam and Eric looked at some of the other projects. There was one called "The Invisible Zoo." It had empty cages and a report on animals that are extinct. There was a scale made from a hot water bottle and a tube. And there was one girl who experimented with her baby teeth. She let the teeth soak in soda. After two weeks the teeth had dark stains.

While Cam read the report "Soda, Sugar, and Teeth," Eric wandered off, looking at other projects. Then he came running back.

"Cam, Cam, where's your camera?"

"It's where I left it, on table 54."

"No, it's not. The folders are there, but the camera is gone."

Chapter Three

Cam ran to table 54. The camera wasn't there.

"Help me look for it," Cam said to Eric.

They looked on the other tables and on the floor. Then, as Cam was looking near a window, she saw a man outside run past. He was carrying something under his jacket and running toward the woods. Cam looked straight at him and said, "*Click.*"

Cam called to Eric. "Come with me. I think whoever took my camera ran outside with it."

Eric followed Cam to the side entrance. No one was out there.

"Let's go back in," Eric said. "Let's tell Ms. Benson. I'll bet it was Linda or her brother who took your camera."

"No. Not now. I just saw a man run from here. Maybe he has the camera. If we hurry, maybe we can catch him."

Cam ran ahead. She stopped running when she reached the edge of the woods. She had seen the man run in there, but now it was dark and quiet. Cam saw a few birds and some squirrels moving in the woods, but nothing else.

When Eric caught up with Cam, she told him to be quiet and listen.

Cam and Eric stood at the edge of the woods for a minute. Then they heard a noise. Cam saw a man move in the middle of the woods. She looked straight at him and said, "*Click.*"

The man turned and saw Cam and Eric. He dropped what he was holding and ran.

"Let's get Ms. Benson," Eric said.

Cam wasn't listening. She was already going into the woods. She tried to run, but she couldn't—too many low branches got in her way. When Cam reached the other side of the woods, the man was gone.

"Did you see which way he went?" Eric

asked when he caught up with Cam.

Cam shook her head.

"Let's go back then."

"No. He dropped something. Let's look for it."

Cam closed her eyes and said, *"Click."* "He dropped it into a big leafy bush next to a tree with white bark, a birch tree," Cam said with her eyes still closed.

Cam and Eric found the birch tree. They searched in the bushes nearby.

"Look! Over here!" Eric said. "I found it! I found your camera! Now we can go back to school."

"But why would someone take it and then throw it away?" Cam asked.

"Maybe he was scared," Eric said.

Cam took the camera from Eric and looked at it. "Whoever took my camera opened it up. I can tell because he didn't put the top on right. Now the film is ruined."

Cam opened the camera. "The film isn't ruined. It's gone!"

Cam sat on the ground. She held the camera in her lap. Eric sat next to her.

"You have your camera back. Why are you so upset?" Eric asked.

"I'm not upset. I'm puzzled. Why would someone want the film in my camera?"

"I still think it was Linda's brother. That Baker family must really love science prizes."

Cam shook her head and said, "No. I don't think Linda or her brother would want to win that way."

Cam sat there and thought for a while. Then she said, "Whoever took the camera must have wanted what was on that film. That's why he took the film and left the camera. But the only picture I took was of you standing next to your sundial. Why would anyone want that?"

Cam closed her eyes and said, *"Click."* She shook her head. Then she said, *"Click,"* again.

"That's it," Cam said and opened her eyes. "I have a picture in my head of you standing next to the sundial. One of the people in the background was leaving a store. He bumped into me and knocked the camera from my hands. He was wearing a red plaid jacket. I think he's the same man I saw in the woods."

"He probably followed us to school," Eric said. "But why?"

"Come on," Cam said. "Let's go back to that store and find out."

Chapter Four

When Cam and Eric reached the bus stop, Cam looked at the row of stores. Then she closed her eyes and said, *"Click."*

"He was leaving a coin store," Cam said. She opened her eyes and pointed to a small shop right behind the bus stop. "That's the one."

They walked to the store. Cam tried to open the door. She couldn't. It was locked.

"There's a sign," Eric said. "It says, 'Collins' Coin Shop. Coins for Collectors. Grand Opening, Monday April 21.' "

"That's next week," Cam said. "Then the store was closed when I took that picture."

Cam thought for a moment. Then she said, "That's it! That explains why that man wanted the film!"

"*What's* it?" Eric asked, but Cam wasn't listening.

She looked through the store window.

"There's someone inside," Cam said, and she knocked hard on the glass.

An old man came to the window. He pointed to the sign and said something. Cam and Eric couldn't hear him.

The old man moved his lips slowly, forming the words, "We're closed."

Cam moved her lips, too. But the man didn't understand what she was telling him.

Cam turned to Eric. "Do you have a pencil and paper?"

Eric took a folded sheet of paper and a pencil from his pocket and gave them to

Cam. "Don't lose the paper," Eric said. "My homework is on it."

Cam turned the paper over and wrote, "I think you were robbed," in large letters. She held the paper up to the store window.

The old man read the note. Then he opened the door and asked, "Why do you think I've been robbed?"

Cam told him about the stolen camera

and the man she saw leaving his store. "Since you were closed, I thought that maybe he robbed your store and stole my camera and the film so that no one would know he was inside."

The man smiled and said, "It couldn't have been this store. The door was locked when I left and it was still locked when I came in. And the alarm was still set. You must have seen him leaving someplace else."

"No. It was this store. It had to be," Eric said. "Cam said, *'Click,'* and when she says that, she remembers everything."

"I don't know about clicks, but I do know I haven't been robbed. Come in and see for yourselves."

It was a small, crowded shop. Locked glass cases with coins in them were hanging along the walls. The old man stood next to a large glass counter. It was filled with coins, old dollar bills, and catalogues.

"I'm Mr. Collins," the old man said. "I've worried that my store might be robbed. The coins in this shop are worth a lot of money. That's why there's a lock on each case and an alarm on the door. Everything here is just the way I left it last night."

Cam told Mr. Collins that she was sorry to have bothered him. Then she and Eric left the store.

As they walked toward school, Eric said, "I still think it was Linda Baker's brother. I'll bet the Bakers have a shelf just waiting for that science trophy."

Cam and Eric stopped at the corner and waited for the traffic light to change. Then, just as they were crossing the street, they heard someone call to them. It was Mr. Collins.

"Come back!" he yelled. "I *have* been robbed!"

Chapter Five

Cam and Eric ran back into the store. Mr. Collins was standing by the door, holding two small display boxes. The boxes were empty.

"These were two of my most valuable coins," he said. "They were gold and almost a hundred years old. And now they're gone."

"Was anything else taken?" Cam asked.

"No. I didn't know anything was gone until I found these empty boxes. They were in the case where I left them. And the case was still locked." He closed the door of the case.

Mr. Collins telephoned the police. Then, after he hung up the telephone, he said to Cam and Eric, "I just don't understand it. I've been robbed and I haven't even opened the store yet. The locks weren't broken."

Cam and Eric stood by the door and waited for the police. Mr. Collins kept shaking his head and saying, "I just don't understand it."

Cam and Eric heard a siren. The noise got louder and louder. Then a police car drove up and parked in front of the coin shop. The siren stopped. Both front doors of the car opened. The driver got out first. It was a tall, thin policewoman. Then a policeman got out from the other side of the car. He was fat and had a mustache. Both police officers came quickly into the store.

The policeman asked Mr. Collins, "What was taken?"

"I don't understand it," Mr. Collins told the police. "I have all the best locks. They're brand-new. I didn't even know I was robbed until these children told me."

"Can you tell us what was taken?" the policeman asked again.

"Two gold coins."

Mr. Collins showed the police the empty display boxes and the case they were kept in. Then Cam and Eric told the police about their science fair and the photograph Cam took of Eric and his sundial.

"A man was leaving this store when I took the picture," Cam said. "He followed us to school and stole the film right out of my camera."

"It's too bad we don't have that picture," the policewoman said.

"But we *do* have a picture of him," Cam told her. "I went, '*Click*,' and took Eric's picture with my mental camera before I used my real camera. I also went, '*Click*,' when the man ran past the window at school and when he dropped my camera in the woods."

"You have pictures! You should have showed them to us right away," the police-man said.

"They are not real pictures," Eric

explained. "They're mental pictures. Cam can look at them and tell you exactly what the man looks like."

The policewoman smiled and said, "That's almost as good."

She took a pencil and pad from her pocket and asked Cam to describe the man.

Cam closed her eyes and said, *"Click."*

"The best picture I have of him is when he ran past the window at school. He was wearing a red plaid jacket, a yellow shirt, and brown pants. He's thin and not very tall. He has dark hair and wears big eyeglasses with red frames."

"What!" Mr. Collins said. "Did you say red eyeglasses? That's Jimmy!"

Chapter Six

"Jimmy? Jimmy who?" both police officers asked Mr. Collins.

"I told you that when I moved in I had new locks and an alarm put in. Well, Jimmy works for the locksmith. Jimmy worked here for almost a week. When he finished, I brought in all these coins. I thought they'd be safe here."

"Where does Jimmy work? What's the name of the locksmith?" the policeman asked.

"He works for Lenny at Sea Side

Hardware. It's in the Hamilton Shopping Mall."

"If you'll come with us," the policewoman said to Cam, Eric, and Mr. Collins, "we'll go there and see if we can find Jimmy."

Cam and Eric got into the back seat of the police car. Mr. Collins locked the front door of his store, set the alarm, and then got into the back seat, too.

The policewoman drove the car into the shopping mall parking lot. She parked it in front of the Sea Side Hardware store.

Cam, Eric, Mr. Collins, and the two police officers went inside the store. Tools and garden supplies filled the front of the store. In the back, behind a counter, there were rows of keys hanging, and a bald man wearing a blue shirt stood there. Along the side of the store were books, magazines, and candy and soda machines.

The policewoman whispered to Cam,

Eric, and Mr. Collins, "Do you see Jimmy anywhere?"

Eric pulled on Cam's sleeve and pointed. Someone with dark hair and eyeglasses with red frames was buying something from one of the machines.

"That's him," Cam whispered to the policewoman.

"Yes, that's Jimmy," Mr. Collins said.

The police walked toward the machines. Cam, Eric, and Mr. Collins followed them.

Jimmy saw the police coming. He looked frightened, but he didn't run off. He turned back to the machine. As he put his money in, Cam looked straight at him and said, *"Click."*

"All right, young man," the policewoman said. "There are a few questions we'd like to ask you and your boss."

They led Jimmy to the back of the store.

"Are you the locksmith?" the police-woman asked the man behind the counter.

"Yes, I'm Lenny."

"Did you put in new locks and an alarm in Collins' Coin Shop?"

"I didn't. Jimmy did. He's new here. It was his first job alone, but I checked his work. He did a fine job."

"Well, the store was robbed. Two gold coins are missing. And these two children saw Jimmy leaving the store when it should have been closed."

"I didn't take any coins. You can check me," Jimmy said.

Jimmy took a pen, a few coins, and some dollar bills from his pants pockets. He put them on the counter. Then he turned his pockets inside out and said, "See, I don't have any gold coins."

Eric pointed to a red plaid jacket hanging behind the counter.

"Can we check your jacket, too?" Cam asked.

Jimmy hesitated for a moment. Then he said, "Sure. Check anything you want. You won't find any gold coins."

Lenny handed the jacket to the policeman. The policeman emptied the pockets. He took out some tissues, chewing gum, and a large ring of keys.

The policewoman picked up the keys. "What are all these for?" she asked.

"Those are my house keys," Jimmy said.

Mr. Collins took a ring of keys from his pocket. He compared the two sets of keys.

"Some of these look just like mine," Mr. Collins said.

Lenny compared the keys and said, "Some of these *are* the same."

44

"All right, Jimmy," the policewoman said, "you'll have to come with us and answer some questions."

"What about my coins?" Mr. Collins asked.

"You're not getting any coins back," Jimmy said, "because I don't have them."

Chapter Seven

Jimmy put his pen and money back into his pockets. Then he put his jacket on.

As the police were leading Jimmy to the front of the store, they passed a man kicking the soda machine. When he saw the police, the man stopped kicking the machine.

"I lost two quarters," he said.

"Well, don't break the machine," the policeman told him as he walked past.

Cam stopped. She looked at the man and

the machine. Then she closed her eyes and said, *"Click."*

She opened her eyes quickly. The police and Jimmy were just leaving the store.

"Stop!" Cam called to them. "Come back here."

The policewoman rushed back. "What is it now?" she asked.

"Just wait here. I think I know where the gold coins are. And," she said to the man, "you'll get your quarters back."

Cam ran to the locksmith's counter. "Someone lost money in the soda machine," she told Lenny.

Lenny opened the cash register and took out some coins.

"No. Don't give him the money. Please, open the machine and see what's wrong."

Lenny took some keys off a hook and followed Cam. He pressed some buttons on the soda machine, but nothing happened. He put a coin into the machine and pressed the buttons again. But still nothing happened.

"When we came in," Cam whispered to Eric, "Jimmy was standing right here. He put something into the machine. It might have been the gold coins."

Lenny unlocked the machine and opened it. Inside were cups ready to slide down a small metal ramp, tubes leading to containers of soda syrup, and a clear plastic coin chute. There were coins stuck in the chute. The first two were gold. Lenny gave the chute a few hard taps and the coins dropped down. Lenny gave the man his money, and he gave the gold coins to Mr. Collins.

"One of these must be bent," Lenny told Mr. Collins. "That's why it got stuck."

Mr. Collins said, "I'm glad. If the coins weren't bent, we might not have found them."

The police drove Cam, Eric, and Mr.

Collins back to the coin shop. Then they took Jimmy to the police station.

"I said before that I didn't know about 'Clicks,'" Mr. Collins told Cam, "but now I do. They help you remember, and they helped find my coins."

Eric looked through the window of the store while Mr. Collins opened the door.

"You may have a good memory," Eric told Cam, "but you forgot about your camera. It's on the counter. We better hurry back to school with it before it's too late to put it in the science fair."

"Don't go so fast. I want to give you something for helping me," Mr. Collins said.

He opened the door. Then he opened one of the cases and took out a handful of coins. He gave five of the coins to Cam and five to Eric.

Eric looked at the coins.

"These are pennies," he said.

Mr. Collins smiled and said, "Yes. If you want to spend them, they're worth just one cent each. But to a collector they're worth much more. These are Indian head pennies, and they're quite old. The last ones were made in 1909."

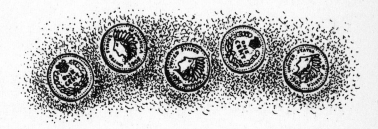

Cam and Eric thanked Mr. Collins for the coins and invited him to the science fair. Then Cam took her camera and walked with Eric to school.

Chapter Eight

That evening Cam and Eric were standing by their projects. Ms. Benson and the other fifth grade teachers walked with the science fair judges from table to table. They asked the children about their projects. Each of the judges wrote notes on a pad. Later they would announce the winner of the science fair.

Cam's parents were at the science fair. So were Eric's parents, his twin sisters, Donna and Diane, and his baby brother, Howie. They all came to Cam's table.

"Did the judges get here yet?" Cam's father asked.

"No, but they'll be here soon. They were just with Eric."

"Do you know what to say?"

"They'll ask me how I made the camera and how it works. And I know all that."

"Don't forget to tell them that the first picture you took was of me," Donna said. "They might think it's Diane because we look alike. You tell them it was me."

The teachers and judges walked up to Cam's table.

"This is Jennifer Jansen," Ms. Benson told the others. "She made a camera. Can you tell us about it, Jennifer?"

"There's no film in it now, so I can open it for you." Cam took the top off the camera. "It started as a box."

Cam showed the teachers and the judges where she put the film and how she had made the shutter with a pin, some tape,

cardboard, and aluminum foil.

"And the most important thing is," Cam said, "that I made sure no light gets into the camera. If light gets in, the film is ruined."

The judges asked Cam some questions.

Then they walked over to the next table.

Everyone waited for the winner to be announced.

Ms. Benson walked onto the stage. She spoke into the microphone while the other teachers and the judges stood behind her.

"Before I announce the winner, I want to thank everyone for coming here tonight. I also want to thank all our fifth grade students for working so hard."

Someone tapped Cam and Eric on their shoulders. It was Mr. Collins. "I hope you both win," he said.

One of the judges handed Ms. Benson a trophy. Then Ms. Benson said, "This year's winner is Joan Cooper for her project, 'Soda, Sugar, and Teeth.' Joan, will you come up here, please."

Eric whispered to Cam, "Well, at least Linda Baker didn't win."

Joan walked onto the stage, and Ms. Benson gave her the trophy. Lights flashed

as her parents and some other people took pictures.

"Why don't you take her picture?" Mr. Collins asked.

"There's no film in my camera."

"No, use your other camera, the one that saved my coins."

Joan was shaking hands with one of the judges. Cam looked straight at her and said, *"Click."* Then Cam looked at Mr. Collins. He was talking to Cam's parents and to Eric and his family.

"I'm taking your pictures, too," Cam told them.

Cam's mother combed her hair. Eric's mother held Howie up so that he would be in the picture. Then they smiled.

Cam looked straight at them all and said, *"Click."*